My Husband, the

Babysitter and Me

Hot Erotic Short Stories Illustrated with

Hentai Pictures

_____

Emily White

TABLE OF CONTENTS

INTRODUCTION

Welcome to a captivating journey where my enthralling stories seamlessly intertwine with enchanting illustrations that redefine the very essence of desire in the world of hentai erotica.

Within the secret pages of these forbidden tales, I invite you to immerse yourself in a fiery universe of unrestrained passion. Every word is a whispered moan, and each illustration is a visual embrace that transforms the realms of fantasy into tangible reality.

This collection is not for the faint of heart. It's a bold manifesto, an invitation urging you to delve into the dark depths of lust, where pleasure is painted with audacious strokes and details that promise to quicken the rhythm of your heart. The illustrations are provocative gateways, guiding you into sensual dimensions where every hidden desire finds its expression without remorse.

Are you ready to plunge into a whirlwind of seduction and temptation, where the pages themselves transform into a stage for your most secret fantasies? Allow yourself to be carried away into a realm where sin transforms into art, and art seamlessly merges harmoniously with the ecstasy of desire.

Lift the cover and prepare for an experience ignited by the flame of passion. This is not just another collection; it's your exclusive ticket to the boldest manifestations of anime eros, written masterfully by me, **Emily White**.

AN EVENING FULL OF SURPRISES

I was a waiter in a restaurant for a year during my studies. A restaurant, with traditional cuisine, with the boss in the kitchen. The clientele consisted mostly of regulars.

I remember one evening when I saw two young women come in. One of them, a blonde with short hair, was not unfamiliar to me. She often came with her husband and two children.

She was hard to forget because she is always dressed in a long full
skirt and a blouse spread over a beautiful chest.

The other, a brunette with big dark eyes, was completely unknown to me. As always, I offered to remove their coats. In fact, my blonde client was wearing a white button-down skirt and a floral blouse. The other was dressed in a dark skirt and a sweater. It was already late in the evening, and I quickly took the order.

Like every time she was there, I couldn't help but stare at her cleavage. It was always at this moment that she met my gaze, and I was surprised to feel myself becoming a peony. They seemed to have plenty of time. As I served them coffee, I saw that one of the skirts had slipped off, revealing a shapely leg clad in stockings.

Since they were my last table and the evening was coming to an end, they asked me for a drink. I sat down at their table and discovered that they were two great friends from childhood. The blonde one's name was Sylvie and the other was Anne, but I didn't find out until later in the evening. We started talking about everything and nothing. Since they didn't seem to be in a hurry and my boss in the kitchen wanted to close up, I suggested they go have one last drink somewhere else. They agreed.

When we left the restaurant, Sylvie suggested we go to Anne's house. So we left in Sylvie's car. On the way, she explained to me that in the small town we were in, it was not serious for two women to have a drink with a young man. It was the same for me. I was sitting up front. Looking at Sylvie, I could see her bare leg. She had white dimples.

She was giving me mischievous looks. So I discreetly put my hand on her knee. She let me. So I moved to her thigh. She eased her thighs a little. I came just above the bottom without difficulty. I felt her flesh when Anne said behind us: "There's our little waiter with wandering hands."

I think she was a little tipsy. Sylvie was, too.

Surprised, I wanted to withdraw my hand, but Sylvie was quicker to put hers on mine and say, 'Stop, you idiot, aren't you okay?

As I spoke to Anne, my hand traveled up her inner thigh to her panties. Sylvie wiggled beside me. When we reached Anne's building, we got out of the car. Anne lived in an apartment on the fourth floor and we rushed up the small elevator, laughing. We were pressed up against each other. I took the opportunity to press myself against Sylvie. She arched her back and couldn't ignore the state I was in. It was going to be a great night. Anne ushered us in. She set us up in a pleasant living room and put on a CD. She told Sylvie to serve us drinks and then left. I was sitting on a deep couch and to get to the bar Sylvie had to walk past me. I grabbed her by the hips and flipped her over onto my lap. She laughed as she wiggled and to shut her up I decided to kiss her. Her mouth was molten lava.

She sucked me in. I took the opportunity to uncover her breasts.

I challenged the buttons on her blouse and began to fondle them. These breasts I had admired so much. They were like two firm apples with two small nipples that I could feel bristling under my fingers.

'So, you two are enjoying yourselves...'.

It was Anne who was looking at us with a smile. She had taken the opportunity to change. She had put on a long shirt that came to her mid-thigh and had the first few buttons open. I could see two small firm breasts.

Can I play with you? I looked at each of them in turn, bewildered. They began to laugh. Anne got down on her knees and removed my shoes before attaching my pants.

Meanwhile, Sylvie removed her blouse and bra and offered me her breasts. My hands were trying to be everywhere at once. I felt Anne's mouth around my cock. She gobbled it up greedily. I had slipped two fingers into Sylvie's sex, who groaned beside me. They got up and took me to Anne's room. A large low bed in front of which Anne pulled up her shirt and knelt, her rump erect. Sylvie took my cock and placed it against her friend's sex. All I had to do was let myself slide into her.

Sylvie put her head behind me while I fucked Anne. She was all wet and came almost immediately. In front of her pleasure, I exploded inside her. Sylvie pulled me out, got down on her knees and buried my cock deep in her throat to lick and suck it. I couldn't take it anymore. She looked at me and said it was now her turn. It was going to be a long and delicious night.

My Husband, the Babysitter and Me

Sylvain, my husband, has waited a long time to allow me to tell you this story. He is standing next to me as I write and is excited that thousands of people will discover a hidden part of our lives. This story begins on a Friday night in July 1996. Sylvain and I had reserved a table in a floating restaurant boat in the middle of a beautiful lake in the region.

Together we had also arranged for a babysitter to watch our son during the evening. As usual, it was a girl from the local high school. Tonight, Alexia was the only one available. We hadn't been going out for a long time, and in truth Sylvain had hidden from me that it was actually going to be a kind of small cruise: on the spot we expected to meet nice couples like ours because we had a secret desire to experience swinging for a long time. This small cruise, organized by a night club, was for us the opportunity not to be missed.

For the occasion, he had also offered me some sexy and daring underwear, like those sold in sex shops. Many readers would like to see me in this outfit. My skirt, all in red latex, barely covered my private parts. By that I mean it was really flush with my sex, waxed for the occasion. For once, Sylvain had advised me not to wear panties, so I wouldn't feel naked in front of men? A small white bodice held my two protruding globes, supported by a tiny bra, with difficulty.

The stares around me, I thought, would become less and less discreet. Everyone, I was sure, would have only one idea in mind: embalm me! Coming out of the bathroom, once I was ready, I walked in front of him a bit, which made him hard.

Inside, I was very happy to have put him in this state. He was starting to grope me. I protested saying that the babysitter would be here any minute but he didn't listen: he wanted to fuck me right now! Really, I wanted to have his big cock in my mouth, but later on the cruise.

I persisted in my refusal and he calmed down a bit. We were at the garage door when a car pulled into the driveway. The driver's side door opened and someone came toward us. It was a neighbor who lived a little further down the street. When he saw me, he was stunned. He had never seen me dressed like this. I felt sort of embarrassed; no one had ever seen me dressed like that. Everyone was calling him Bob.

I smiled at him and asked him what I could do for him. He responded with a big smile and looked at me and said he'd rather not tell me how I could help. He complimented me on my attire and said he wished his wife was that hot. I thanked him for the compliment, but explained that I needed to leave right away. He was silent for a while, but continued to stare at me.

I got in the car and turned red when I realized that Bob had gotten a good view of my smooth pussy. He said he was looking for his dog who had run away. I closed my door and rolled down my window as Bob got closer and closer. He was standing in front of me, my face level with his zipper.

I couldn't see his face but I knew what he was looking at. The top of his pants, in front of me, was beginning to bulge. My breasts, pressed into the bodice, were almost sticking out of my bra. My nipples were hard and visible. Suddenly I stuck my head out. He stepped back just in time. I had almost pressed my right cheek against his crotch. I told him I hadn't seen his dog and that I really had to go. He thanked me and hurried back to his car. I was sure he was going to masturbate.

Alexia arrived at 7:15. She was waiting on the front porch and already running in our direction. She whistled when she noticed my outfit and admitted that she found me really hot. This compliment, coming from an 18-year-old girl, made me very proud.

She asked me how Sylvain found me. I told her how he had wanted to rape me earlier in the house. She gave a little giggle and blushed. Alexia was a very sweet girl. We talked like old friends. She easily told me about her adventures with her boyfriends and it wasn't unusual for us to talk about sex. That night I felt like my outfit gave her some ideas.

She said she was a virgin, which surprised me greatly. I gave her instructions for the night: television for our son, what time she was supposed to put him to bed, etc. We had been driving for quite a while, but the weekend traffic was very difficult. A few miles from the lake, our headlights dimmed excessively, so we had to push the car to the side of the road.

A passing highway repairman called his station and was willing to help us. Sylvain and he fiddled under the hood for a while and after 10 minutes the car started up again. We already knew that the boat had not waited for us. We thanked the mechanic after paying him. Sylvain and I decided to go home after this incident.

However, once in the hallway, I started to hear strange noises coming from the room. I could hear the moans of more than one person. It was certain that these noises were coming from people having sex. More curious than scared, I slowly walked towards the door. I didn't know whether to continue or go back to the kitchen. I was already imagining Alexia being filled by one of the young guys circling her and I could see her pumping a young small cock.

I went back to the kitchen where I told Sylvain everything and he told me, surprised, that he had no idea who it could be. We thought it would be fun to walk slowly over to them to find out more. As for me, inside I thought that Sylvain didn't want to miss the opportunity to take advantage of an 18-year-old girl and that this idea alone motivated him.

Once we were close to the room, we could hear the boy saying a lot of bad words to her.

We could hear him moaning through the wall. But suddenly, the voice we heard was really that of another girl. But who was it?

Sylvain smiled at me and gently pushed open the door: our little babysitter was simply watching one of our personal videos.

In fact, Sylvain, during some of our exchange nights, takes his camera. Alexia, Sylvain whispered to me, was sitting on the floor, her shorts and panties next to her. She was watching the television intently, one hand slipping into her crotch, rubbing her little pussy furiously.

On the screen you could see my sister, Gina, like a real whore, being fucked by Sylvain. While her boyfriend, a black man, was pinning me to the floor with his big cock in my pussy.

Sylvain and I were stunned, standing by the door, not knowing what to do. Wasn't Alexia about to tell the whole neighborhood about our filmed adventures? We decided to enter the room. Alexia had two fingers in her pussy that she often put in her mouth. She didn't notice our presence, carried away by her pleasure.

Sylvain, entering the room, began kneading my breasts, overwhelmed by the spectacle. He had reached the front of my bodice and was pulling out my breasts, massaging one of the erect nipples. I could feel his cock stiffening through his pants. Alexia was a beautiful brunette with already beautiful breasts, larger than mine.

As Sylvain pulled out his cock and lifted my skirt, Alexia turned around and said mellifluously 'Oh, my God'. Without breaking stride, Sylvain continued to pull up my skirt, spread my legs and fucked me dry, while the babysitter watched in amazement. The latter remained petrified, not daring to say a single word, her eyes fixed on our lustful couple.

As Sylvain unloaded into my ass and withdrew exhausted, Alexia began to speak. 'Excuse me,' she said, 'I'm sorry...' She was really confused. Suddenly she came up to me and started crying. I could feel her young warm body, her round and firm breasts on my chest.

As she wrapped her arms around me, her fingers encountered a few drops of cum left on my skirt. I advised her to put her clothes back on, but all she did was pull up my skirt and caress my butt.

She looked me in the eye and asked if Sylvain could get her drunk like in the movie she was watching. Sylvain looked at me with great complicity.

I had her on all fours, keeping only her shirt on, with her ass erect. Sylvain took his cock in his hand and directed it first toward the babysitter's mouth. He seemed to swallow it almost whole. She immediately started sucking like a real whore would.

This girl must have been watching our videos. As she demanded it in her pussy, Sylvain withdrew and brought his cock close to her virgin vulva. Methodically he began the penetration. Alexia let a few cries escape, but quickly ran his tongue over her mouth.

She was already demanding more and demanded that Sylvain fill her deeper, which he did without being asked. After two minutes, he began raking in earnest so that she ended up squirming in all directions. Sylvain, aroused as always, cried out that he was coming.

Alexia then begged him to come and burst in her mouth. She had just seen my sister Gina on the screen, pumping and swallowing Sylvain's cum and wanted to do the same. Immediately a rain of cum poured down her throat.

The little slut swallowed it all and ran her tongue over her lips, taking care to look at us, as if to ask us to evaluate her performance. On the television screen that had been left on, we could see a close-up of me being filmed from both sides by my brother-in-law accompanied by Sylvain while Gina held the camera.

We were silent in front of the television for a while until the movie ended. Alexia got up first. We offered to drive her home and the three of us were in the front seat of the car five minutes later. When we arrived in the parking lot of her house, she naturally leaned over Sylvain and gave him a blow job while reaching for my nose with her unoccupied right hand. The car was starting to smell like cum. Alexia obviously wanted Sylvain to spray her again.

After a good fifteen minutes of pumping my husband, our little babysitter finally got what she wanted: under pressure, some of the cum dripped down her chin as Sylvain unloaded. Again, she swallowed it all, readjusted, gave us both a kiss, and ran off in the direction of her apartment.

THE BEACH

I've always loved taking a walk by the sea in September. There are no more tourists, and you can better appreciate the vastness of the ocean.

And it's usually still warm, especially in the mid-afternoon. I remember one particularly hot day. It was a few days before school started. I was walking through the dunes as usual and thinking about school, all the homework, the friends. I was entering fourth grade, a class that is considered difficult.

It was really hot and I decided to go for a swim. Since there was absolutely no one around, I stripped completely off my clothes and ran to the sea. I swam for a good half hour. On the way out, a cool wind forced me to run to the dunes for shelter. It was warm again; I lay on my back without dressing and fell asleep.

I was awakened by the sound of voices and muffled laughter. Still numb, I preferred not to open my eyes and wait for the intruders to leave. The whispering noises began again. This time, a little more awake, I was able to estimate the distance.

They were girls' voices, which must have been about ten yards away. I waited for them to leave while continuing to pretend to be asleep. The voices began again. This time they were really close. I could make out what they were saying.

- Come on, let's get a little closer. - You're crazy, what if he wakes up? - But come on, we'll see better. This time I was completely stunned, I didn't dare to breathe. My heart was pounding.

- Look at his big dick. The giggles and whispers were now close. I felt a shadow pass over my face. The crunch of sand told me they must be sitting right on my lap. My arms began to shake.

- Look how beautiful he is, naked. - Stop it, you'll wake him up. - But no, look. I felt a small warm breath along my penis. My heart was starting to race. The two girls burst out laughing.

- You are completely crazy. They laughed again. I felt a brush of hair on my testicles followed by a small kiss on my glans. Their laughter indicated that she was as excited as I was. I still didn't move.

- Look, her dick is getting bigger by the minute. - Come on, let's go. - No, wait... This time it was a hot, wet tongue that began to roam around my glans. My penis became very hard.

- Wow, it's huge. It's turning me on.

- Yes, I am too...

After she held back a laugh, one of them put my penis in her mouth. I could feel her tongue wandering around my organ and it was very hard to hold back my orgasm.

Shy at first, her mouth swallowed more and more of my sex. A shudder of air told me that his girlfriend had just dropped her clothes and tossed them next to me. The shadow on my face told me that she had placed herself right on top of me. She was straddling my head and brought her pussy up to my nostrils.

Her breath was warm, turning me on.... I was itching to lick her clit, but then I would give myself away. So I just breathed harder. Her pussy was now in contact with my nose and she began to rub against it. Her sex, which was as soft as a baby's skin, became very wet.

Meanwhile, the first girl had stopped sucking me and it was her turn to undress. She took my penis and tried to direct it to her slit. After the third attempt, my cock entered her hot vagina.

She started to walk on top of me. I couldn't take it anymore, but I didn't want to cum inside her. She had to be young and probably not on the pill. The pleasure she was giving me was becoming unbearable....

- Let's switch... - Okay... It was time: as my penis left her bowels, I couldn't hold back my ejaculation.

- Oh, hell... I didn't even like it.

They laughed. I heard them put their clothes back on and walk away, holding back their laughter. Still dazed from this adventure, I didn't open my eyes immediately. When I finally sat up, my belly was covered in my seed. Next to me was a pair of flowered panties left behind by one of the two girls.

I picked it up to wipe my belly and caress myself with it. It was late and I hurried to get dressed and go home. To this day, when I think about that story, I can't help but get an erection.

WEEKEND IN THE SUN

My name is Frank, I'm 21 years old and I live in Aix en Provence where I'm a student. It is a beautiful and lively city and connoisseurs will not mind. My parents have a villa in the suburbs, which means I don't have to rent a place to live. I may be less independent, but the financial aspect is not to be neglected.... On the other hand, my parents, enjoying their retirement very efficiently, are always traveling and that leaves me a lot of time, living alone in the house. It's a nice house, comfortable, with a pool, everything....

I have two friends who are really nice. They are Sabrina, my girlfriend, and Corinne, her best friend.

I have been dating Sabrina for 6 months. We liked each other right away and she didn't hesitate to give herself to me shortly after we met. Our first steps in bed were a little difficult, since it was the first time for both of us. We didn't know how to approach our desires, our cravings. Until the day we realized that we should not be ashamed or afraid to talk about it.

From that moment on, it was wonderful. In fact, we are truly complicit, both of us, in our lovemaking and especially in the mutual confession of our fantasies. We both want more and more, and we both give more and more. Each of our sexual encounters resembles a game, a real game, that of love.... And this mutual complicity seems to me to be the cement of a really solid and lasting relationship. So we really enjoy it, knowing full well that time passes too quickly.... Sabrina has a "temperament" and knows very well how to fulfill herself sexually. She also takes great pleasure in bringing me with a lot of cheerful mischief into her web, which I happily get lost in.

Corinne is more discreet, less jovial, but just as beautiful and well-built as Sabrina. Her experiences in love, according to Sabrina, have been unfortunate, having so far only fallen in love with selfish, inconsiderate, no-contact guys, totally blinded by their pleasure, their enjoyment, their performance, their dick...

Once again, my parents are away again, and have left me the house, recommending that I take care of it. So I take advantage of the fact that my mother has restocked the refrigerator before her departure, to invite Corinne and Sabrina to come and spend the weekend with me. They enthusiastically accept and it is on Saturday morning that they both show up with their things. They were cheerful, laughing at nothing, not wasting a second putting their things in their room. Sabrina will sleep in mine, which is normal, and Corinne will go to the big guest room.

As soon as they arrived, they were in their bathing suits in the pool. No problem!!! All in the water! And so we have fun all afternoon. Diving, sunbathing, playing in the water, talking, joking, teasing each other. The three of us are fine, we're safe from trouble, and we're having fun. Sabrina is adorable as can be, not refusing, on this convivial afternoon, a sweet caress, even giving me one under Corinne's discreetly absent gaze. But I'm sure she lacks nothing....

And then I noticed that, when they are both alone, they never stop giggling and making low masses. Their complicity is also a pleasure to watch, but it is absolutely impossible for me to know what they are talking about. Girl talk...certainly.

In the evenings, they volunteer to do the cooking, which, while very simple, is still presented with tasteful and thoughtful delicacy poolside. Paradise...

As evening falls, after the meal, we take another dip in the lighted pool. The girls are lovely in the illuminated water.

- What about skinny dipping?

That's an idea I'm considering....

- Yes, great!" says Sabrina, excitedly.

And in the water, she takes off her bathing suit and tosses it to me while I'm still sitting on the shore.

I enjoy admiring it for a few seconds. Then I stand up, take off my bathing suit and quickly dive in without thinking too much to get closer to Sabrina. And we hug very lovingly. She whispers in my ear, amused:

- Hey! You're going to get in trouble if you keep....

She's absolutely right.

- Corinne! Are you coming with us?

Sitting down on a chair, she dries off.

- No thanks, I'm not used to it yet...

- Let's go! Take off your shirt!" encourages Sabrina! It's really nice! I assure you, you won't regret it!

I also insist. In the water, we approach her to decide.... And, oh surprise, she gets up, leaves her swimsuit quickly, modestly, and rushes into the water, to join us. She seems to enjoy it, as she rolls and turns and jumps in the water, like a child.

Then we get out, drying quickly, because the air lacks sunshine.... This sudden nudity doesn't seem to bother too much. As far as I'm concerned, I'm doing well... but I'm far from showing it off like I might after a cold shower. It has to be said that the girls both have nice little butts... which draws my gaze quite involuntarily.... And since I don't know Corinne's! The attraction of the new...

Once we're dressed, we head home. I want to go to my room with Sabrina and after saying goodbye, we leave Corinne in front of the TV.

In the bedroom, while Sabrina is washing herself in the bathroom, I ask her:

- Tell me, Sabrina, do you know Corinne well? Has she ever had sex?

- Yes, I think so... Why do you ask? Are you interested?

- No! That's not why I'm asking. I just want to know where she is sexually, and if we don't shock her too much sometimes....

- Oh, well then, don't worry about her...

- What do you mean?

- You know, Corinne confides in me a lot. It's true that she's quite concerned about sexual matters at the moment, but she's careful and patient. I know she hasn't had much luck so far... She has only met idiots... Yet she is a lively girl who doesn't refuse anything when the opportunity arises....

- Is that so? Explain yourself!

She comes back into the room, naked, and lies down on the bed, her hair still wet.

- Well, you see, last month, at my house, we bought ourselves an extra....

- What do you mean? Did you sleep with her?

- No! But you see, she had found some sex magazines among her father's things. She was quite disturbed by them, physically. She definitely wanted to show them to me. I have to admit, I like them. So we both, sitting on her bed, flipped through them. And then the desire grew. Without hesitating for a second, I asked her if she felt like masturbating. With naive frankness, she didn't hesitate a second to answer in the affirmative.

So I encouraged her to do it...just like that, in front of me! You see, I had never seen a woman caress herself before. A little embarrassed, she agreed to do it on the condition that I also do it at the same time as her.... Why not! So we both enjoyed masturbating in front of each other, in all simplicity, one eye on the magazines, but the other on the performance we were giving each other.... She showed me her pleasure, I showed her mine and I assure you we had a great time! It was really good!

- I can't believe it! Corinne, who does that!

- And you know, I liked it too.... So we did it again the next day... in the shower in the bathroom.... It was great!

- And did he touch you?

- No, not at all! It was just to show us our pleasure.... We both had fun, that's all! Is there anything wrong with that?

And now I was walking on thin ice:

- Tell me, Sabrina... How would you like it if we made love... both of us to her?

A pensive silence from which the devil or reason would come out! She confessed with the utmost sweetness:

- I don't know, I never thought of it.... But now that you tell me... Why not?

And suddenly, looking more determined:

- But do you think he'll take it well?

- To find out, all you have to do is try... and then we'll see... there's no risk in trying... Do you agree?

- Come against me, my pig...

She's adorable, lying on the bed like that... That evening, I made love to her with great tenderness, sensing that something would happen soon... and that Corinne would soon share our lives... intimately.... Also, Sabrina, perhaps voluntarily, was not very discreet when we made love and I'm sure Corinne heard everything!

The next day, Sunday, we wake up around 11am. Breakfast on the terrace by the pool, in our bathing suits. The sun is shining. The girls have prepared a good breakfast and we enjoy it. Everyone is in a good mood. Corinne is cheerful and Sabrina continues with her little game of whispers and laughter, full of smothered secrets. They are really enjoying themselves and are a pleasure to watch. They must be talking about last night....

Then it comes time for a swim. Sabrina doesn't ask anyone anything and gets naked. The other girl does the same; I am obliged to follow her. Later, while standing in the shade, I find it hard to remain impassive as I admire the girls, side by side, lying on their stomachs, naked, sunbathing. Their small shapely buttocks, the arch of their loins, all of it does not leave me indifferent and I am forced to dive very quickly into the water to calm myself. On their mats, they giggle. It must amuse them...

I can feel that something is going to happen, but I don't really know what or how it's going to happen.... Besides, this is all so new to me....

That evening, the weather turns cloudy and it even starts to rain. We take shelter in the large living room. I am wearing a t-shirt and Bermuda shorts and the two girls are wearing a short dress with thin straps that shows off their breasts, which are not constricted by unsightly bras.

We decide to watch a video. It's Sabrina going through my dad's tapes....

- Wow! Look what I found! An X-tape!

- Oh yes, exclaims Corinne! We're going to have a good laugh!

I ask her:

- Do you like to watch sex?

And in a tone of derision:

- Look at it...who doesn't like to look at asses? Everybody likes it... You don't like it?

And he insists that we watch it. After all, why not?

I grab the remote and sit down in one of the chairs. The two girls collapse on the couch, munching on pistachios. The movie starts and we get into it a little too quickly for my liking. The girls giggle, whisper things in each other's ears, laugh, sometimes out loud. On the screen, asses, asses.... But how badly these movies are made! No plot, no atmosphere. As I watch the video, I watch them out of the corner of my eye. Corinne seems more fascinated than Sabrina, whom I catch looking at me. We exchange a knowing glance.

Gradually, the film unfolds without much interest, although one scene, despite everything, is quite well shot. It shows two women doing a guy in a car, in the back seat, under the eyes of voyeur men masturbating behind the window. Nothing special per se, but for once, very well shot.

The girls whisper confidences in each other's ears.... I see Sabrina looking at me with a curious look. I can sense that they are up to something between them.... Corinne herself asks me to backtrack to review this scene. Once the encore is over, Corinne looks more and more fascinated.

Sabrina winks at me, like a signal, and gets up to stand next to me. With great tenderness she takes my head and holds it to her stomach. My right hand rests on the inside of her thighs and I caress her knee. Her skin is soft, very soft. Corinne, sitting cross-legged on the couch, stares at the screen, still fascinated. Without being seen, my hand goes up with great tenderness and softness. I feel a strong pressure of her hands on my head. And I discover with my fingertips that she is not wearing panties. I immediately have an erection. Embarrassed, I innocently place my left hand on my sex to keep my glans from obscenely lifting my shorts from the inside.

A quick glance at Sabrina lets me know she's noticed. She's smiling happily, ready to continue.... My fingers touch her hair and very discreetly, without Corinne noticing, I slip a finger between the lips, wet as ever, of Sabrina's sex. She closes her eyes, half-closing, not daring to give in to the pleasure completely. This discreet masturbation, under Sabrina's dress, accentuates my erection even more and I don't know how to hide it.

Corinne's fascinated look at the scene on the screen is suddenly disturbed by a significant sigh that Sabrina cannot contain. Staring at a pistachio, she stares at us incomprehensibly at first, not believing her eyes. Sabrina, still standing next to me, had opened her legs slightly and I couldn't help but grab my sex through my Bermuda shorts, thus showing, to Corinne's astonished gaze, my swollen bra!

- Wow!" she exclaimed. This is amazing!

She has put down her packet of pistachios and, still sitting cross-legged, looks at us steadily, showing little interest in the TV, from which only sighs and cries of pleasure are coming out. My right hand is now penetrating Sabrina with two fingers, and she has positioned herself with her legs open enough to give herself the pleasure movements of her pelvis on my fingers. Her hands resting on her knees, she indulges in the caress of my fingers, giving her pelvis these obscene but apparently very pleasurable movements.

- You... Are you... Corinne asks me in a hesitant voice....

I nod and show her with my eyes the impressive and unmistakable deformation of my shorts.

- Wow, she has an erection! It's nice to look at you! I've never seen... Wow, that really turns me on, you know....

- Well, jerk off!" sighed Sabrina.

- So, right in front of you," she said surprised!

- And then, what are we doing?

- Just like that!

And she sinks her hand under her dress, without showing us anything.... I can see her hand wiggling under her dress and her eyes starting to look strange. Sabrina, on the other hand, continues to take her foot on my finger.

Corinne, who is beginning to surrender to the pleasure, has rolled onto her side on the couch, knocking over the package of pistachios. She's always giving us a voyeuristic look.... Her eyes code, she's really enjoying herself... and she whispers to me between two sighs:

- Oh Frank, it feels good... it feels good to do it in front of you two.... I feel like I'm going to cum... in front of you! Frank! Do me a favor: jerk off too.

I don't need to be told twice!

I leave Sabrina for two seconds and she takes advantage of the free moment to pull her dress over her head. Hastily, I leave my Bermuda shorts on and sit back down, my shaft free, hard and erect toward the ceiling. Also naked as a worm, Sabrina kneels beside me, her gaze greedy. She grabs my shaft and starts stroking it. Corinne's eyes are almost glassy. Her hand gets stronger and stronger under her dress, and her eyes roll over and over again....

So I'm enjoying being provocative:

- Corinne, calm down! Take a good look!

I generously wet my hand and begin to slide the glans between my fingers. She watches, fascinated.

- Yes! ... She's jerking off...

Sabrina, with her head resting on the forearms of the armrest, is also watching, amused. She's up to something, because she gives Corinne a characteristic look, as if she's about to offer her something. It doesn't take much.

- Corinne! Come, come closer! Come take a closer look!

Corinne stops masturbating, slides to her knees on the carpet and sits on her heels in front of me, facing my open legs. She stands there, not knowing what to do but watching us, watching me masturbate gently, accompanied by Sabrina's knowing gaze.

- Come on! Take off your dress!

Unhurriedly, she pulled it over her head! She was also naked under her dress. It was Sabrina who encouraged her:

- Well, let's go! Don't be afraid! ... Come closer and do to her what you've been dying to do for a long time.... That's it, isn't it?

I ask him:

- Is this your first time?

She nods, looks at me and looks at Sabrina. Sabrina has taken my cock from my hands and is masturbating it in turn.

- Watch closely!" she says.

And she puts her lips on his glans as if to give him a big kiss. I feel his tongue wetting the tip and my glans is soon caressed by two moist lips. He pulls back, still holding me and invites Corinne!

- Come on, come and have some fun... with the most beautiful toy in the world....

Corinne nods, laughs, gets up on her knees, crosses the necessary few inches, puts her two hands behind her back and leans on my cock, well held by Sabrina, her lips kiss...

The contact is soft, it seems to be pleasant for her.... I also feel her tongue running over the tip of my glans. She stops, raises her head, satisfied with this first feat, and starts again, savoring the seconds present.

Sabrina and I watch her enjoying herself. She closes her eyes in pleasure. Then her lips suddenly open. I feel a soft warmth invade my sex. Corinne has pushed it all the way down my throat, holding me in place, swirling her tongue around it, causing a sudden rush of desire.... In turn, I close my eyes, moaning, surrendering to this caress, thrusting my pelvis forward.... He loosens his hands, which so far have been held behind his back, and takes my shaft with a firm, determined hand, beginning to masturbate me with amplitude, with attention, with application, his eyes full of stars...

- Is this how you do it? asks Sabrina....

With a willing and protective gesture, Sabrina replies:

- Yes! We do this and much more! Watch!

She slowly gets up and straddles me with her back to me, resting her hands on my knees. Corinne was holding my sex in her hand. She understood immediately. Sabrina, looking intently at her lower abdomen, slowly reaches down to her taut bra, until she touches it with the tip of her vaginal lips. Corinne plays with my sex on Sabrina's vulva, caressing it.... She bursts out laughing...

And Sabrina rises slowly, pushing my meaty rod deep into her vagina, her eyes closed as she sighs in relief... I still feel a soft warmth invading my glans. Corinne is there, her eyes inches from the union of the two sexes. I can see her on her side. She is stroking herself, looking very carefully, not missing a beat.... Sabrina begins to move up and down, thrusting into my sex with increasing violence and force. She starts to cum, screams, sighs, blows, puts her hand on Corinne's head, who stands there, fascinated.

Sabrina falls backwards, lying on top of me, offering Corinne the spectacle of her well-filled pussy. Corinne admires this tube of flesh, sinking, coming out, sinking.... Then, as if gripped by a huge need for sexual tenderness, she brings her face closer to both sexes and forcefully places her lips on Sabrina's vulva, giving her all the juices and kisses in the world, inserting her tongue into every possible nook and cranny, feeling under her lips the base of my glans in an almost extended position. I feel the warmth of her mouth, her lips. An abrupt exit from Sabrina's sex sends me deep into Corinne's mouth, but it doesn't matter. It's hot, it's good, and Sabrina is on cloud nine...and silently comes hard, both on my sex and in Corinne's mouth.

With her head to one side, she kisses me, as if to thank me, and then stands up, leaving me standing there with my erect sex. She leans toward Corinne:

- Come on! Come on... it's your turn now! You'll see... everything will be fine.

- Do you think so? Can I do it?

A little hesitantly, he gets on top of me, facing me this time, and sits on my thighs. We look into each other's eyes and I sense a great sweetness. Slowly, our faces meet and our lips meet, and she becomes furious in her kiss. I calm her down! stroking her shoulders and her breasts that are in front of my nose.... I bury my face in them... this makes her laugh again....

I look over at Sabrina. She's sitting next to me in the chair, one leg on the armrest, quietly masturbating, winking at me.

Corinne slides her pelvis onto my sex. Her vulva is wet and she strokes my bandaged sex, resting on my stomach. She rubs against it, stroking herself with my sex, without me penetrating her. It is a very pleasant caress. We both look down at our bellies. Hers is flat, muscular, young and moving a lot! Between her thighs my glans appears, then disappears, regularly, turgid, swollen with desire, purple!

It is Sabrina who launches, her mouth distorted with pleasure:

- So, are you putting it in, Corinne?

Corinne lifts up a little, adjusts my sex herself, and slowly descends. I sink into her as if in bliss, with no resistance. It's warm, it's soft, it's great. And we stay there, completely encased, without moving, drinking each other in with our eyes and stomachs, flooded with desire and pleasure. Then, slowly, he begins a slow, imperceptible movement of his pelvis. He closes his eyes, isolates himself in growing pleasure, and of course uses me as his object of pleasure. And so do I... I hold her on my hips and it's wonderful!

She moans:

- Oh!... This is amazing... How good it feels... oh yes!....

And she continues to thrust her pelvis, enjoying completely, almost bestially my sex pressed into hers, to get the maximum pleasure from it. She thrashes with regularity, aware of the pleasure she gives me as she draws her own pleasure from my meaty rod. She is performing true masturbation with my sex as she would with a dildo. I look over at Sabrina. With her thighs wide open, she has inserted two or three fingers into her vulva and is masturbating frantically, her eyes half-closed, feasting on us. I invite Corinne to look at her. She forgets her pleasure for two seconds and turns her head towards Sabrina.

- Oh yes, Sabrina... it's okay...

Corinne holds out her hand, inviting her to join us. Sabrina gets up, kneels behind Corinne, puts her arms around her stomach, caresses her breasts and kisses her on the neck.... Corinne surrenders to this soft, tender caress as I plunge into her. But in my position, I can't move much.... To my surprise, it's Sabrina who gives Corinne the amplitude of movement that makes me jerk... lifting her slightly but regularly...

- Look at my darling, she whispers in her ear.... We're going to make him cum... He's about to spit it all out...

- Wait, not yet... Let me come first...

As she says this, a wave of pleasure floods her, and without really knowing why, Corinne screams her pleasure as she digs her nails into my shoulders, frantically wiggling her pelvis on my sex in an almost casual manner. Her face grimaces, screaming mute in invisible pain.... Then he calms down... slowly emerging, regaining his senses, looking at me tenderly and kissing me very tenderly before turning his head and kissing Sabrina in turn...

- How good it was! I've never come so hard! It's great what you're doing for me, you know....

And she gets out of the way. I sit there, with my sex fully erect. Sabrina kneels down next to me and starts playing:

- Come on, Corinne, go the other way.... Let's make him come, our little man.... Hein Frank! You want us to give you a good hand job?

And turning to Corinne, he continues:

- And it really turns me on... Have you ever seen a guy squirt?

- No, I have to admit I haven't.... well, not like we have now!

- So, you'll see, he'll do it to us, just for the two of us.... Isn't that right, my dear?

As he did so, he grabbed a small bottle of Tahitian oil, "monoi". He had already prepared this for me. It is delicious. The two girls sit on their knees on the carpet, on either side of my knees. Their breasts touch my thighs.... I reach out and caress them both.... It feels amazing! Sabrina pours some oil into her hand, puts the bottle back down and with a jovial and amused smile, bathes my penis with this delicious oil that smells good on my still erect penis...

The caress is indescribably delicious.... His hand slips very gently, slowly, his eyes in mine to see the effect. She plays with my glans between her fingers, squeezing it quite hard and passing it between her phalanges very gently. She invites Corinne to do the same. Corinne, in turn, grabs my shaft, and with a more curious look than Sabrina's, repeats the same gestures....

-Wow, that's great....

Her eyes are like those of a child who discovers a new toy: amazed and full of projects... She looks at me too, to see the effect. I surrender completely to this divine masturbation, offering my irreversible erection to the fingers or hand of one of them, it doesn't matter. My hands grope their breasts, titillate the tips.

- Come a little closer, girls, so I can jerk you two off too....

They are not told twice. Slightly turned towards me, one on my right, the other on my left, still on my knees, I can stick a finger into their wet pussy...really wet. And it doesn't take long for the results to kick in.

Corinne is the first to launch... as she jerks me off....

- Oh! it's coming back! I'm about to go again... Oh, it's so nice to do this with you two.... Frank, Sabrina, I'm about to come again....

-Go ahead my dear, Sabrina replies to him, her mouth already distorted with pleasure, her eyes half closed. I'm coming too... You'll see how it will squirt...

And she caresses my balls while Corinne's fingers are still working greasily around my glans, which is about to burst... They both accentuate my caress by moving their pelvises, getting off on my fingers without any embarrassment or modesty...

- Oh girls! This is fantastic! I'll send it all to you as soon as possible....

- Are you the one who makes him come? asks Sabrina to Corinne, between two sighs....

- Oh yes... I'd love to....

- Then I'll do something he likes, my little Frank...

And while Corinne masturbates me with an increasingly confirmed dexterity, while on my side my fingers caress two wet vulvas, Sabrina approaches my anus with her fingers...

- Oh yes... this is really good....

Aided by the large amount of oil that has dripped from her hand, she has no problem gently forcing my anal muscle... I feel her finger digging in very gently and I begin a sort of truly divine anal masturbation. Prompted by Sabrina on this side and Corinne on my glans, I totally surrender to the pleasure they give me, thanking the heavens for putting me there, tonight, in their hands... expert hands applying themselves, making me give the best of myself... It is the height of pleasure to be able to give myself totally from my lower belly to these hands full of vice and without any virtue, brazenly determined to make me spit out my orgasm without any restraint or embarrassment...

The pleasure rises, rises...

- Look, Corinne, I'm giving him a hand job... He likes it, the bastard!

- And me, I feel it coming soon... It's fun... I can feel him getting harder and harder between my fingers....

My breathing becomes more and more anarchic, my sighs more and more hoarse. I know I only have a few seconds left before I give in, but I put off this sublime moment as long as I can... Eyes fixed on my glans, the two girls are waiting for the moment when everything will come out.... Corinne masturbates faster and faster, obviously taking her foot on my finger, Sabrina floods my anus with too rare sensations, which will contribute to my near ejaculation...

I try to restrain myself... Realizing this is the moment, they watch my meatus, from which, without warning, one, then several spurts of semen are violently expelled, crashing into Corinne's hair, onto Sabrina's forehead. Corinne emits a hoarse cry of victory and, without waiting, takes my sex naively into her mouth, while I am still ejaculating with much less vigor, swallowing with undisguised pleasure the last drops of semen still trapped...

Sabrina asks for some too, and they both lick my cock clean of my dripping cum.... Suddenly, in their lip-smacking frenzy, their mouths come together, perhaps not quite by Hazard. They make a surprisingly slobbery, swirling spit as they finish each other off on my fingers, breathing heavily and awkwardly through their noses... They cum together, eye-to-eye, as if they're discovering each other, in this lesbian kiss.... Then they let their joy, their joie de vivre, explode....

- Wow, that was amazing! exclaims Corinne! And you, Frank?

I emerge... completely stunned, like after a hurricane! Slowly... I stroke their hair, draw their faces to mine and we kiss generously...

all three of us... with much softness... pleasure... tenderness... and love... yes... just love!

GO TO THE BEACH

This was the first time I had ever had this experience. Some friends had told me about it. I had seen reports on TV. I was thinking about it.

When Sandra suggested that I spend the afternoon on this naturist beach, I was really hesitant. But then I plucked up the courage. I called Sandra. I told her it was okay, that I wanted to come, but that I wouldn't promise anything about stripping.

It's 2:30 p.m., it's really hot, Sandra and I get to the beach, there are a lot of people, nudists and not. Sandra leads me to a quiet place. We put down our towels between a lonely guy, quite young, not very handsome, but naked, completely naked, and a group of girls, in swimsuits.

I have to tell you, I'm 19 and I haven't seen many naked guys in my life, so my beach neighbor was bound to catch my attention.

After putting down my towel, I take off my tank top revealing my cute swim top. Then I take off my skirt, revealing the matching bottom. I might even say that at the price this swimsuit had cost me, it was all the more reason to keep it.

Sandra took off her shirt, revealing her breasts.

It was the first time I had ever seen her breasts. They were quite small but very pretty. I was a little embarrassed to look at her breasts and not very excited...the feelings were mixed.

Then she takes off her shorts. She is wearing a small white thong. I keep staring at her, she must think I'm an idiot. Then, of course, she goes ahead and takes off the thong.

So, I was already embarrassed when I saw her beautiful breasts, I can't tell you when I saw her sex. She had a perfectly shaved pubis.

I was even more confused. I thought I had breasts three times the size of hers and that I hadn't waxed at all, or at least not that much. I didn't know if I would go any further. I was hesitant. Sandra wasn't paying attention to what I was looking at.

- Are you keeping your shirt on?

- Well, I don't know, I'm not used to it....

That's right, I don't know, I'm not used to it.

- At least take off your shirt!

I don't know what to do, but I don't want to look like an idiot in Sandra's eyes. So I take off the top at 44. This is the first time my breasts are exposed to so many people. I am terrified and at the same time very excited, especially when I look at my neighbor....

- He seems to like you," says Sandra, referring to the neighbor in question.

- Do you think so too?

- Yes, go ahead, approach him, go talk to him....

I manage to overcome my embarrassment to take off my bra, I don't know if I can move.

Still, I get up and walk towards this boy. He must be 18-19 years old.

- Do you want to go for a swim? I ask him.

- Well, yes, he replies, obviously intimidated.

Once in the water, he relaxes a bit.... we're in the water up to our necks, so we're fully clothed again.

He tells me:

- Do you come here often?

   - No, this is the first time.

- And you didn't dare go all the way....

- Well, no...

I'm a little ashamed... so I tell you:

- But I haven't gone yet...

- Let's see if you're that brave.

- I'm ready...

- Give me your bikini bottoms

After hesitating for a moment, I hand him my swimsuit bottoms, thus finding myself completely naked, but in the water, no one could see him...

- Wait for it!

He came out of the water to put my swimsuit on and returned a few minutes later.

- There, now you can't go back....

- That's right," I said to myself.

Suddenly, I feel him approach me, grab me by the waist and slide a hand lower.... I feel him brush against my pubic hair.... I'm terribly aroused.

- Make love to me! I order him...

He takes my hand and places it on his hardened penis.... I start to caress him... moving closer to him... his hands go all over my body, he goes to my breasts, my sex, and he doesn't hesitate to venture a finger inside...

We continue our caresses, when suddenly, I see Sandra enter the water.

She probably hadn't seen anything of our little maneuver, hadn't seen her come out in my bathing suit, and I didn't want her to see me groped like that.

- Wait, let me go for five minutes, my girlfriend is coming....

She does this as Sandra swims towards us.

- Hi handsome, so are we trying to pervert my girlfriend?

- Not really... she answers shyly.

Suddenly, she dives under the water, towards our new friend's sex.... She starts smiling with pleasure, I don't even dare to imagine what she's doing underwater. Suddenly, she approaches.

- But where is your bikini bottom?

I was very embarrassed...and still very excited.

Sandra leads us to a small deserted bay. We arrive on the sand... getting out of the water is a great moment, I reveal to everyone (well Sandra and this young man) my brown hair and he can't hide his erect penis.

We lie on the sand, he lies on his back, so Sandra comes and sits on his penis. The penetration is deep and Sandra starts moaning as soon as he starts moving.... I, on the other hand, begin to envy her and let one hand go to my sex. As she gets turned on by this stranger, I do the same with my hand....

Seeing me like this, Sandra gets up and walks over to me. She pushes my hand away and replaces it with her tongue. Her tongue gently wanders over the surface of my sex, spreads the labia majora, touches my clitoris, I feel I'm about to explode, she slides a few fingers into my vagina. I'm fed up, my fingers have been slipping out for an hour, I want something else....

But she doesn't stop, and soon I explode with a loud scream. A powerful orgasm surges through me. And in turn, I impale myself on our friend, as her tongue gives Sandra immense pleasure.

Since Sandra had prepared him well, he soon comes. The jet is so strong that it triggers another orgasm in me...he pulls out, and I empty myself of an impressive amount of cum. Sandra, while continuing to be touched, lies down in the direction of the pool of cum that has formed on our friend's belly and licks it off. She then begins to lick his penis, slowly, then faster, then takes it into her mouth.

Watching this scene, I feel the desire rise in me again, and I throw myself in turn on our shared penis. While I polish his glans, Sandra takes care of his testicles, quickly he ejaculates again, covering my hair with his natural glue....

I want to cum again, I ask him to penetrate me, but he can't take it anymore....

- I'm dead, I can't do anything more...

And in fact his penis is slowly falling off... it must be said that it has been well taken care of.

Sandra has gone back into the water to rinse off a bit, I'm there on the sand, my hair full of cum and in my right hand the softened penis of a stranger to whom I didn't dare show a breast two hours before.